Geronimo Stilton
ENGLISH!

10 WELCOME TO MY HOUSE! 歡迎來我家！

新雅文化事業有限公司

www.sunya.com.hk

Geronimo Stilton English
WELCOME TO MY HOUSE! 歡迎來我家！

作　　者：Geronimo Stilton 謝利連摩·史提頓
譯　　者：申倩
責任編輯：王燕參
封面繪圖：Giuseppe Facciotto
插圖繪畫：Claudio Cernuschi, Andrea Denegri, Daria Cerchi
內文設計：Angela Ficarelli, Raffaella Picozzi
出　　版：新雅文化事業有限公司
　　　　　香港筲箕灣耀興道3號東匯廣場9樓
　　　　　營銷部電話：（852）2562 0161
　　　　　客戶服務部電話：（852）2976 6559
　　　　　傳真：（852）2597 4003
　　　　　網址：http://www.sunya.com.hk
　　　　　電郵：marketing@sunya.com.hk
發　　行：香港聯合書刊物流有限公司
　　　　　香港新界大埔汀麗路36號中華商務印刷大廈3字樓
　　　　　電話：（852）2150 2100　傳真：（852）2407 3062
　　　　　電郵：info@suplogistics.com.hk
印　　刷：C & C Offset Printing Co.,Ltd
　　　　　香港新界大埔汀麗路36號
版　　次：二〇一一年六月初版
　　　　　10 9 8 7 6 5 4 3 2 1

版權所有·不准翻印
中文繁體字版權由Atlantyca S.p.A. 授予
Original title: LA MIA CASA
Based upon an original idea by Elisabetta Dami
www.geronimostilton.com

Geronimo Stilton names, characters and related indicia are copyright, trademark and exclusive license of Atlantyca S.p.A. All Rights Reseved.
The moral right of the author has been asserted.

Stilton is the name of a famous English cheese. It is a registered trademark of the Stilton Cheese Makers' Association.
For more information go to www.stiltoncheese.com

No part of this book may be stored, reproduced or transmitted in any form or by any means, electronic or mechanical, including photocopying, recording, or by any information storage and retrieval system, without written permission from the copyright holder. For information address Atlantyca S.p.A., via Leopardi 8 - 20123 Milan, Italy - foreignrights@atlantyca.it - www.atlantyca.com

ISBN: 978-962-08-5366-1
© 2007 Edizioni Piemme S.p.A., Via Tiziano 32 - 20145 Milano - Italia
International Rights © 2007 Atlantyca S.p.A. - via Leopardi, 8, Milano - Italy
© 2011 for this Work in Traditional Chinese language, Sun Ya Publications (HK) Ltd.
9/F, Eastern Central Plaza, 3 Yiu Hing Rd, Shau Kei Wan, Hong Kong
Published and printed in Hong Kong

CONTENTS
目 錄

BENJAMIN'S CLASSMATES
班哲文的老師和同學們

Maestra Topitilla
托比蒂拉・德・托比莉斯

Rarin
拉琳

Diego
迪哥

Rupa
露芭

Tui
杜爾

David
大衛

Sakura
櫻花

Mohamed
穆哈麥德

Tian Kai
田凱

Oliver
奧利佛

Milenko
米蘭哥

Trippo
特里普

Carmen
卡敏

Atina
阿提娜

Esmeralda
愛絲梅拉達

Pandora
潘朵拉

Takeshi
北野

Kuti
菊花

Benjamin
班哲文

Hsing
阿星

Laura
羅拉

Kiku
奇哥

Antonia
安東妮婭

Liza
麗莎

老鼠記者精英會
Geronimo Stilton English Club

參加表格

成為會員，可參加英語培訓課程，以及暢遊世界各地學英語，包括香港、歐洲、美加等。

同時成為新雅書迷會會員，更可享以下優惠包括：

★到指定門市及書展可獲購書優惠　　★最新優惠及活動資訊
★收到會訊《新雅家庭》　　　　　　★參加有趣益智的書迷會活動

請填妥此表格傳真或郵寄至新雅文化事業有限公司市場部 (傳真號碼及地址載於背頁)

□ 本人已是新雅書迷會會員 (編號：SY＿＿＿＿＿＿＿＿＿＿＿)

□本人現想申請成為老鼠記者精英會及新雅書迷會會員。

姓名＿＿＿＿＿＿＿＿＿＿＿＿＿＿＿＿＿＿＿　性別：＿＿＿＿＿

出生日期：＿＿＿＿年＿＿＿月＿＿＿日　年齡：＿＿＿＿

日間聯絡電話：＿＿＿＿＿＿＿＿＿＿＿＿＿＿＿＿＿＿＿

學校：＿＿＿＿＿＿＿＿＿＿＿＿＿＿＿＿＿＿＿＿＿＿＿

電郵：＿＿＿＿＿＿＿＿＿＿＿＿＿＿＿＿＿＿＿＿＿＿＿

職業：□ 學生　□ 家長　□ 教師　□ 其他＿＿＿＿＿＿＿＿

教育程度：□ 小學以下　□ 小學 (＿＿ 年級) □ 中學 (F.＿＿)
　　　　　□ 大專　□ 其他

從哪本書獲得此表格：＿＿＿＿＿＿＿＿＿＿＿＿＿＿＿＿＿

地址 (必須以 **英文** 填寫)：＿＿＿＿Room(室)＿＿＿Floor(樓)

＿＿＿＿Block(座)＿＿＿＿＿＿＿＿＿＿Building(大廈)

＿＿＿＿＿＿＿＿＿＿＿＿＿＿＿＿＿＿Eastate (屋邨 / 屋苑)

＿＿＿＿Street No.(街號)＿＿＿＿＿＿Street(街道)

＿＿＿＿District(區域)HK/KLN/NT* (*請刪去不適用者)

以上會員資料只作為本公司記錄、推廣及聯絡之用途，一切絕對保密。

PLEASE STAMP HERE

請貼上郵票

新雅文化事業有限公司

老鼠記者精英會
Geronimo Stilton English Club

香港筲箕灣耀興道 3 號
東滙廣場 9 樓

新雅文化事業有限公司
SUN YA PUBLICATIONS (HK) LTD

www.sunya.com.hk

查詢電話：(852)29766559

傳真號碼：25074003

GERONIMO AND HIS FRIENDS
謝利連摩和他的家鼠朋友們

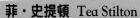

謝利連摩・史提頓 Geronimo Stilton

一個古怪的傢伙，簡直可以說是一隻笨拙的文化鼠。他是《鼠民公報》的總裁，正花盡心思改變報紙業的歷史。

菲・史提頓 Tea Stilton

謝利連摩的妹妹，她是《鼠民公報》的特派記者，同時也是一個運動愛好者。

班哲文・史提頓 Benjamin Stilton

謝利連摩的小侄兒，常被叔叔稱作「我的小乳酪」，是一隻感情豐富的小老鼠。

潘朵拉・華之鼠 Pandora Woz

柏蒂・活力鼠的姨甥女、班哲文最好的朋友，是一隻活潑開朗的小老鼠。

柏蒂・活力鼠 Patty Spring

美麗迷人的電視新聞工作者，致力於她熱愛的電視事業。

賴皮 Trappola

謝利連摩的表弟，非常喜歡食物，風趣幽默，是一隻饞嘴、愛開玩笑的老鼠，善於將歡樂傳遞給每一隻鼠。

麗萍姑媽 Zia Lippa

謝利連摩的姑媽，對鼠十分友善，又和藹可親，只想將最好的給身邊的鼠。

艾拿 Iena

謝利連摩的好朋友，充滿活力，熱愛各項運動，他希望能把對運動的熱誠傳給謝利連摩。

史奎克・愛管閒事鼠 Ficcanaso Squitt

謝利連摩的好朋友，是一個非常有頭腦的私家偵探，總是穿着一件黃色的乾濕褸。

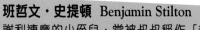

WELCOME TO MY HOUSE!
歡迎來我家！

親愛的小朋友，把你的約會通通取消吧，今天可是個大日子！為什麼？很簡單啊，就像喝一杯雪梨乳酪奶昔一樣那麼簡單……我想邀請你來我家作客呢！我以一千塊莫澤雷勒乳酪發誓，今天我們要一起學習有關房間啊、傢具啊，以及房子裏所有東西的英文名稱，我相信你一定會學得很開心的。準備好了嗎？一起來吧！

have a look 看一看
come in 進來

Hi! Would you like to see my house?

Come in. Let's have a look first outside and then inside.

跟我謝利連摩‧史提頓一起學英文，
就像玩遊戲一樣簡單好玩！

你可以一邊看着圖畫一邊讀。
以下有幾個標誌，你要特別留意：

🧀 當看到 💿 標誌時，你可以聽CD，
一邊聽，一邊跟着朗讀，還可以跟
着一起唱歌。

🧀 當看到 ⭐ 標誌時，你可以和朋友
們一起玩遊戲，或者嘗試回答問
題。題目很簡單，它們對鞏固你所
學過的內容很有幫助。

🧀 當看到 ❗ 標誌時，你要注意看一
下格子裏的生字，反覆唸幾遍，掌
握發音。

最後，不要忘記完成小測驗和練習
冊裏的問題！看看你有多聰明吧。

祝大家學得開開心心！

謝利連摩‧史提頓

THIS IS GERONIMO'S HOUSE
這是謝利連摩的房子

歡迎你來到我的家！我非常非常愛我的家。你看，我的家從外面看起來是不是很大很漂亮呢。現在請你先跟班哲文和潘朵拉一起用英語說出下面的詞彙吧！

A SONG FOR YOU! Track 1

Geronimo's House

Geronimo's house is very nice,
very nice, very nice,
Geronimo's house is very nice
yippee, yippee, yeah!
Geronimo's house is very big,
very big, very big,
Geronimo's house is very big
yippee, yippee, yeah!
Geronimo's house is very funny,
very funny, very funny,
Geronimo's house is very funny
yippee, yippee, yeah!

balcony

Open the window.

wall

Close the window.

roof

chimney

window

door

letter box

bricks

handle

key

lock

doormat

bush

This is the key of the door.

⭐ 1. 試用英語説出以下的
詞彙：門、門墊、
把手。

⭐ 2. 鑰匙、鎖用英語該怎
麼説？説説看。

2. 鑰匙：key，鎖：lock。
handle：把手
1. 門：door，門墊：doormat。
答案：

THE HALL, THE DINING ROOM AND THE KITCHEN
玄關、飯廳和廚房

接着，我請大家進屋裏參觀，柏蒂口渴了，我連忙到廚房倒了杯水給她喝。從大門到廚房要穿過飯廳。在廚房的旁邊還有洗衣房和雜物房。讓我帶大家參觀一下吧……

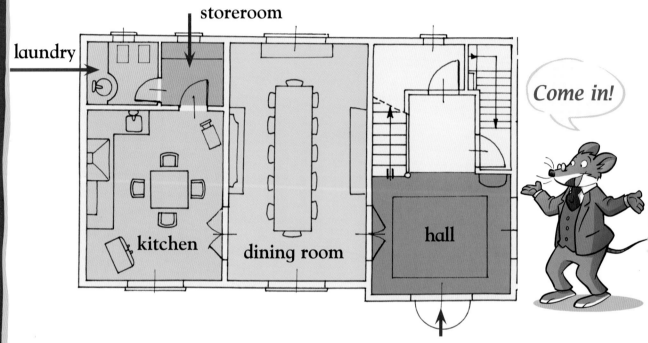

每個房間裏都有不同的傢具和裝飾品。班哲文和潘朵拉好奇地指着每一件東西，並說出它們的名稱，當然是用英語啦！你也跟着一起說說看。

In the hall you can see:

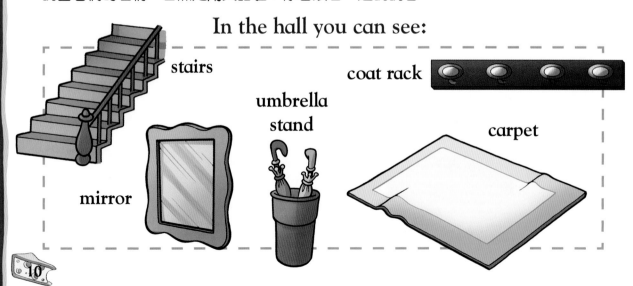

In the dining room you can see:

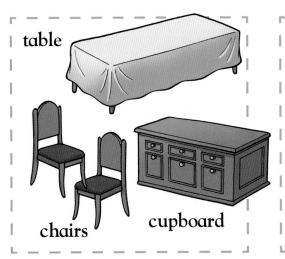

table

chairs

cupboard

In the kitchen you can see:

fridge

cooker

oven

tap

dishwasher

sink

In the laundry you can see:

clothes-horse

washing machine

laundry basket

In the storeroom you can see:

broom

cloth

hoover

bucket

ladder

⭐ 回答下面的問題，正確的就説「Yes, it is.」，
錯誤的就説「No, it isn't.」。

1. Is the coat rack in the hall?
2. Is the cupboard in the dining room?
3. Is the fridge in the laundry?

Yes, it is. *No, it isn't.*

1. Yes, it is.　2. Yes, it is.　3. No it isn't.

答案：

THE LIVING ROOM AND THE STUDY 客廳和書房

我家的客廳很典雅，而且光線充足。客廳裏還放着一座鋼琴，潘朵拉和班哲文對鋼琴很感興趣，他們可不會放過任何彈鋼琴的機會啊。這個時候，柏蒂正在教他們用英語說出客廳裏的東西的英文名稱……你也跟着一起說說看。

In the living room you can see:

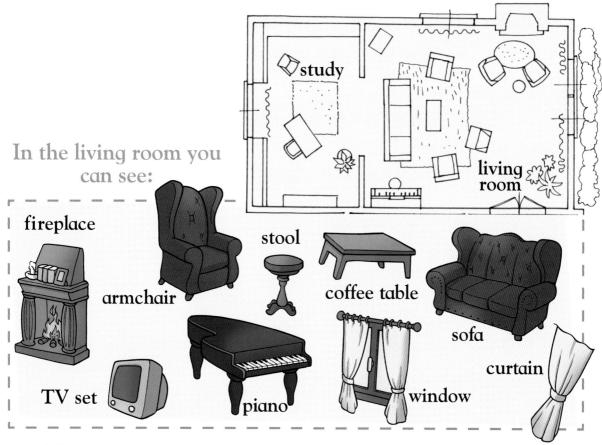

fireplace

armchair

stool

coffee table

sofa

TV set

piano

window

curtain

接着，我帶大家來到書房參觀，書房裏很安靜，放滿了書和報刊，還有一張舒適的椅子和一張書桌。班哲文和潘朵拉想知道怎樣用英語說出書房裏的東西的名稱，例如書櫃、枱燈、電話……你也跟着一起說說看。

In the study you can see:

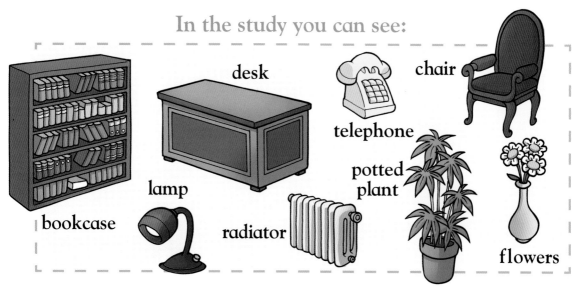

desk

chair

telephone

potted plant

bookcase

lamp

radiator

flowers

⭐ 1. 鋼琴在哪裏？請用英語說出來。

⭐ 2. 電話在哪裏？請用英語說出來。

答案：
1. The piano is in the living room.
2. The telephone is in the study.

BENJAMIN'S PLAYROOM
班哲文的遊戲室

在我家的二樓有一間專為班哲文而設的遊戲室,他來我家的時候就會在這裏玩。班哲文已經迫不及待要給潘朵拉看他所有的玩具了……哇,遊戲室裏的東西真多呢,這些東西的名稱用英語該怎麼說呢?你也跟着一起說說看。

⭐ 看看班哲文的遊戲室,你最喜歡的東西是什麼呢?請用英語回答。

encyclopedia

poster

computer

crayons

plasticine

dictionary

This room is really beautiful!

This is my playroom, Pandora!

microscope

puzzle

paints and brushes

radio-controlled car and plane

football

marbles

tennis ball

"Snakes and Ladders"

14

SNAKES AND LADDERS 康樂棋

　　潘朵拉在班哲文的遊戲室裏看到一副棋子，她覺得很好奇。這副棋子叫做「康樂棋」，很多小朋友都懂得玩……你也想一起玩嗎？遊戲的規則很簡單！

FINISH

| | football | | tennis ball | |
| 23 | 24 | 25 | 26 | 27 |

| | | microscope | | 18 |
| 22 | 21 | 20 | 19 | |

| | dictionary | | radio-controlled car | |
| 13 | 14 | 15 | 16 | 17 |

| brushes | | | puzzle | | crayon |
| 12 | 11 | 10 | 9 | 8 | 7 |

| | plasticine | | computer | | marbles |
| 1 | 2 | 3 | 4 | 5 | 6 |

START

遊戲玩法：

✽參加者輪流擲骰子，然後按照骰子上顯示的數字，移動棋子。

✽當參加者的棋子停在一個有英文詞彙的格子裏，他就要把這個英文詞彙讀出來，並用中文說出它的意思。如果說錯了，下一輪就要罰停一次。

✽如果棋子停在有梯子和蛇圖案下面的格子裏，就可以順着蛇梯爬到上面的格子去；如果棋子停在有梯子和蛇圖案上面的格子裏，就要順着蛇梯滑到下面的格子去。

✽最先到達FINISH的參加者為勝。

GERONIMO'S BEDROOM
謝利連摩的睡房

潘朵拉想看看我的睡房，於是我打開了睡房的門，讓她看看。睡房裏擺設得井井有條，真不錯！我還教她和班哲文用英語說出睡房裏的物品的名稱，你也跟着一起說說看。

GERONIMO'S BATHROOM
謝利連摩的浴室

我經常說好主意都是在浴室裏想出來的，所以大家都很好奇想看看這個地方。班哲文和潘朵拉還一邊參觀，一邊學習用英語說出浴室用品的名稱呢，你也跟着一起說說看。

bathrobe

shower gel

shower

mirror

shampoo

soap

washbasin

| have / take a bath | 洗澡 |
| have / take a shower | 淋浴 |

towel

I have a bath every day.

bathmat

I take a shower every day.

sponge

toilet

bathtub

slippers

toilet paper

試用英語說出：「我每天都洗澡。」

答案：I take a bath every day.

17

THE GUESTROOM 客房

我的家還有一間客房，裏面有一張小牀。潘朵拉趁機問柏蒂房間裏一些物品的英文名稱該怎麼說，你也跟着一起說說看。

LET'S GO DOWNSTAIRS!
到樓下去！

參觀完各個房間後，現在大家都下樓回到了客廳。班哲文迫不及待地想跟我們玩一個遊戲，你也一起來玩吧，看看你能不能回答他們的問題。

Where is the bed?

It's in the bedroom.

Where is the armchair?

It's in the living room.

Where is the fridge?

It's in the kitchen.

Where is the washing machine?

It's in the laundry.

A SONG FOR YOU!
Track 2

A Coloured House

In my bedroom
I have a carpet,
a yellow carpet,
a yellow carpet.
In my bedroom
I have a bed,
a blue bed, a blue bed.
In my bathroom
there is a shower,
a red shower, a red shower.
In the kitchen my sink
is pink, is pink.
Yellow, pink, red and blue,
this is the house for you!
In my dining room I have a
table, a green table, a green table.
In the living room the armchair
is blue, is blue.
Yellow, pink, red and blue,
this is the house for you!

upstairs 樓上
downstairs 樓下

19

〈五鼠齊喝茶〉

班哲文和潘朵拉在班哲文的遊戲室裏，玩得十分開心。

班哲文：我們再來玩一次康樂棋吧！

潘朵拉：好啊！我喜歡玩這個遊戲！

當潘朵拉和班哲文在玩康樂棋時，謝利連摩正在他的書房裏看書。

The doorbell rings...

Who can it be?

I don't know. Let's go find out!

這時，門鈴響了……
班哲文：會是誰呢？
潘朵拉：不知道呀，我們出去看看吧！

Who is it, Uncle Geronimo?

I don't know. I'm going to see!

班哲文：謝利連摩叔叔，是誰來了？
謝利連摩：不知道呢，我正要去看看。

Hello! Aunt Lippa, please come in!

Hello! Come on Benjamin, it's time to go home!

Please let me stay a little bit longer!

謝利連摩：你好，麗萍姑媽，請進來！
麗萍姑媽：你好，來吧！班哲文，是時候回家了！
班哲文：請你讓我多留一會兒吧！

Geronimo persuades Aunt Lippa to stay a little longer. He asks her to take a seat in the living room while Benjamin and Pandora go back to the playroom.

Thank you Geronimo! You're very kind!

Aunt Lippa, this way, please!

謝利連摩說服了麗萍姑媽多留一會兒，他請姑媽到客廳裏坐下來，而班哲文和潘朵拉則回到遊戲室裏繼續玩耍。
謝利連摩：麗萍姑媽，這邊，請！
麗萍姑媽：謝謝你，謝利連摩！你真好！

謝利連摩：這次會是誰呢？我去看看。

賴皮：你好，謝利連摩！我突然想來見見你！
謝利連摩：賴皮……你剛好趕得及下午茶時間呢！

賴皮的肚子很餓，所以他徑自向廚房跑去。

麗萍姑媽：我正想去廚房沖一些茶……
賴皮：現在是下午茶時間嗎？怪不得我的肚子餓了！

賴皮：你需要我幫忙嗎？

麗萍姑媽：不用了，賴皮，我自己做就行了。

可是賴皮不聽麗萍姑媽的話，他把廚房弄得一團糟。

麗萍姑媽：賴皮，看看你做了什麼！

謝利連摩：賴皮，你真是笨手笨腳！看看你把這裏弄得一團糟，我要怎樣才能打掃乾淨呢？

麗萍姑媽：不用擔心，謝利連摩，我會幫你收拾乾淨的。

The End

謝利連摩：來吧，大家一起來吧！雖然廚房裏一團糟，但是下午茶已經準備好了！

班哲文和潘朵拉：下午茶？我們來了，謝利連摩叔叔！

23

TEST 小測驗

⭐ 1. 用英語説出以下的詞彙：

| 磚 | 屋頂 | 煙囪 | 窗子 | 門 | 信箱 |

⭐ 2. 你還記得家裏這些地方用英語怎麼説嗎？説説看。

| 浴室 | 飯廳 | 廚房 | 睡房 | 雜物房 |

⭐ 3. 你還記得在謝利連摩的客廳和書房裏有些什麼物品嗎？請用英語説出來。

⭐ 4. 你還記得在班哲文的遊戲室裏有些什麼物品嗎？請用英語説出來。

⭐ 5. 用英語説出以下的句子。

(a) 我們可以出去露台嗎？　　　　**(b)** 這幢房子真漂亮啊！

⭐ 6. 你還記得謝利連摩家的房間是怎樣分布的嗎？試用英語回答，如果房間在樓下就説 downstairs，如果在樓上就説 upstairs。

(a) Where is the dining room?　　**(b) Where is Benjamin's playroom?**

(c) Where is Geronimo's bedroom?　　**(d) Where is the kitchen?**

DICTIONARY 詞典

（英、粵、普發聲）

A

alarm clock　鬧鐘

armchair　扶手沙發

B

balcony　露台

bath　洗澡

bathmat　浴室足墊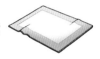

bathrobe　浴袍

bathroom　浴室

bathtub　浴缸

bedroom　睡房

bedside table　牀頭櫃

bedspread　牀罩

blanket　毛毯

bookcase　書櫃

bricks　磚

broom　掃把

brushes　畫筆

bucket　水桶

bush　灌木叢

C

carpet　地毯

chest of drawers　衣櫃

chimney　煙囱

cloth　布

clothes-horse　晾衣架

clumsy　笨手笨腳

coat rack　衣帽架

coffee table　茶几

computer　電腦

cooker　煮食爐具

cosy　舒適的

crayons　蠟筆

cupboard　櫥櫃

curtains　窗簾

D

desk　書桌

dictionary　詞典

dining room　飯廳

dishwasher　洗碗碟機

doorbell　門鈴

doormat　門墊

E

encyclopedia　百科全書

F

fireplace　火爐

floor　地上

flower pot　花盆

fridge　雪櫃 (普：冰箱)

G

glasses　眼鏡

go back　回去

guestroom　客房

H

hall　玄關 (普：門廳)

handle　把手

hoover　吸塵機

hungry　肚子餓

I

inside　裏面

J

just　剛好

K

kitchen　廚房

L

ladder　梯子

lamp　燈

laundry　洗衣房

letter box　信箱

light bulb　燈泡

living room　客廳

lock 鎖

look at 看着

M

marbles 彈珠

mess 一團糟

microscope 顯微鏡

mirror 鏡子

myself 我自己

N

nice 好

O

outside 外面

oven 焗爐

P

paints 顏料

piano 鋼琴

pillow 枕頭

plasticine 泥膠

playroom 遊戲室

poster 海報

potted plant 盆栽

puzzle 拼圖

R

radiator 暖爐

railings 欄杆

ready 準備好

rocking chair 安樂椅

roof 屋頂

S

shampoo 洗髮水

sheet 牀單

shower 淋浴 / 淋浴間

shower gel 沐浴露

sink 水槽

sit down 坐下來

slippers 拖鞋

soap 肥皂

sofa 沙發

sponge　海綿

stairs　樓梯

stool　矮凳

storeroom　雜物房

study　書房

T

tap　水龍頭

telephone　電話

tennis ball　網球

this way　這邊

tidy up　收拾

together　一起

toilet　馬桶

toilet paper　廁紙

towel　毛巾

U

umbrella stand　雨傘架

W

wall　牆

wardrobe　衣櫃

warm　溫暖

washbasin　洗臉盆

washing machine　洗衣機

window　窗子

看在一千塊莫澤雷勒乳酪的份上，你學得開心嗎？很開心，對不對？好極了！跟你一起跳舞唱歌我也很開心！我等着你下次繼續跟班哲文和潘朵拉一起玩一起學英語呀。現在要說再見了，當然是用英語說啦！

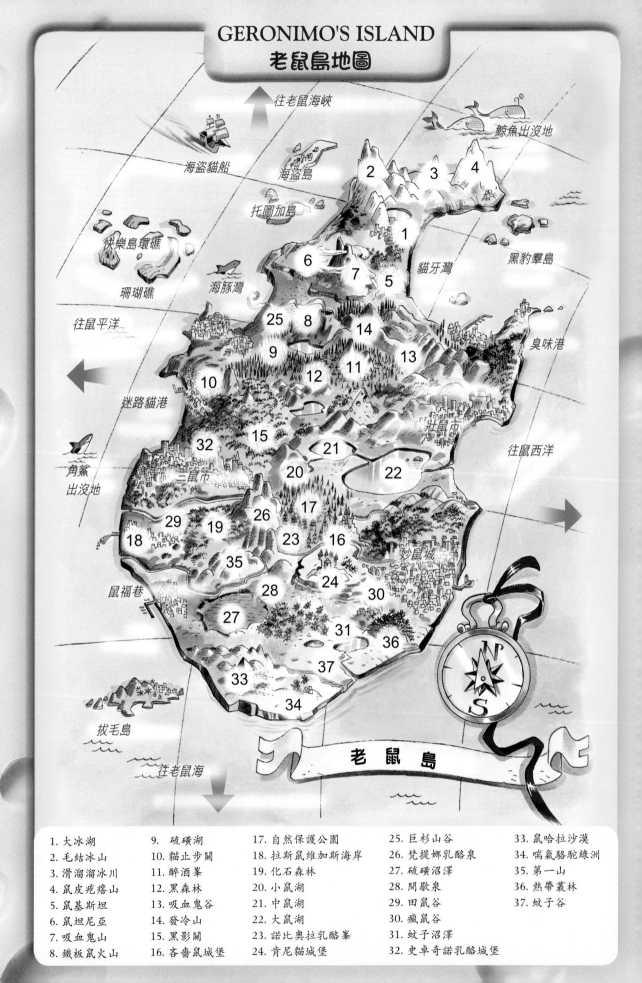

GERONIMO'S ISLAND
老鼠島地圖

往老鼠海峽

鯨魚出沒地

海盜貓船

海盜島

托圖加島

黑豹羣島

快樂島環礁

珊瑚礁　　海豚灣

貓牙灣

臭味港

往鼠平洋

迷路貓港

往鼠西洋

角鯊
出沒地

壯鼠市

三鼠市

妙鼠城

鼠福巷

拔毛島

往老鼠海

老鼠島

Geronimo Stilton

EXERCISE BOOK
練習冊

想知道自己對 WELCOME TO MY HOUSE! 掌握了多少，
趕快打開後面的練習完成它吧！

ENGLISH!

10 WELCOME TO MY HOUSE! 歡迎來我家！

DRAW AND WRITE
畫一畫、寫一寫

⭐ 1. 把下圖中的虛線連起來，畫出謝利連摩家的窗戶，然後給圖
　　畫填上顏色。

⭐ 2. 從下面選出適當的字詞填在橫線上。

(a) Downstairs there are _____ .

> three windows　　two windows　　four windows

(b) Upstairs on the first floor there are _____ .

> three windows　　two windows　　four windows

YES, IT IS. NO, IT ISN'T.
是的，它是。不是的，它不是。

⭐ 根據下面的問題，把正確的答案填上顏色。

1. Is the fridge in the kitchen?

Yes, it is.　　No, it isn't.

2. Is the washing machine in the laundry ?

Yes, it is.　　No, it isn't.

3. Is the cooker in the storeroom?

Yes, it is.　　No, it isn't.

4. Is the dishwasher in the hall?

Yes, it is.　　No, it isn't.

5. Is the table in the dining room?

Yes, it is.　　No, it isn't.

6. Is the chair in the kitchen?

Yes, it is.　　No, it isn't.

WRITE THE WORDS 寫一寫

⭐ 根據下面的圖畫，選出正確的詞彙填在橫線上。

dining room	kitchen	storeroom
bathroom	living room	study

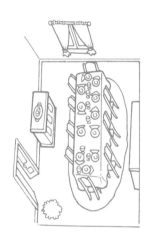 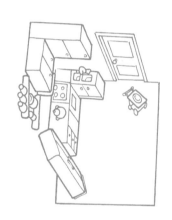 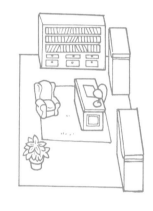

1.＿＿＿＿＿＿＿　　2.＿＿＿＿＿＿＿　　3.＿＿＿＿＿＿＿

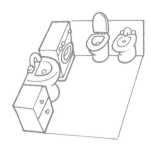  

4.＿＿＿＿＿＿＿　　5.＿＿＿＿＿＿＿　　6.＿＿＿＿＿＿＿

MATCH THE WORDS TO THE PICTURES 配對

⭐ 班哲文的遊戲室裏有些什麼？在各圖畫旁的空格內填上代表答案的英文字母。

A. marbles　　B. microscope　　C. dictionary
D. radio-controlled car　　E. tennis ball
F. football　　G. paints and brushes
H. computer　　I. crayons　　J. plasticine

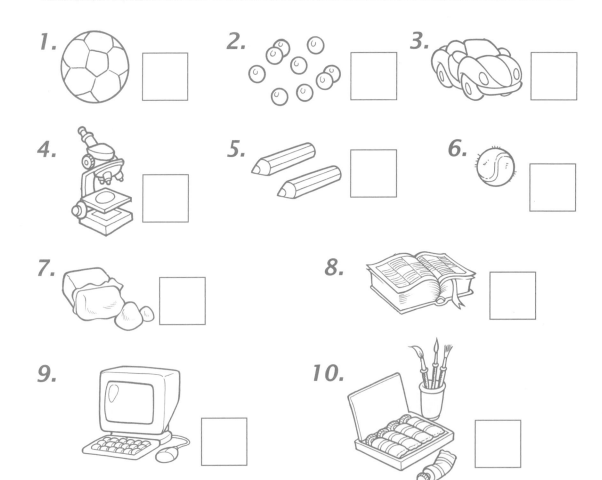

TRUE OR FALSE 判斷對錯

⭐ 判斷下面的句子，如果是正確的就在橫線上寫上true，如果是錯誤的就在橫線上寫上false。

1. The bed is in
   the bedroom.

   _____

2. The bedside table
   is near the bed.

   _____

3. The pillow is
   under the bed.

   _____

4. The bathtub is
   in the bathroom.

   _____

5. The desk is in
   the bathroom.

   _____

6. The shower is in
   the bathroom.

   _____

READ AND DRAW
讀一讀、畫一畫

 讀出下面的句子，然後根據句子的內容畫出物品。

1.

Draw a potted plant in the living room.
Draw a carpet on the floor.

2.

Draw a telephone on the big table and a TV set on the small table.

3.

Draw a lamp on the bedside table.
Draw a pillow on the bed.

WRITE AND READ
寫一寫、讀一讀

⭐ 從下面選出正確的詞彙填在橫線上，完成句子，然後把句子朗讀出來。

| piano | bookcase | playroom | bed |

1. The _____ is in the living room.

2. The books are in the _____ , in the study.

3. There's a single _____ in the guestroom.

4. There is a carpet in Benjamin's _____ .

ANSWERS 答案

TEST 小測驗

1. bricks   roof   chimney   window   door   letter box
2. bathroom   dining room   kitchen   bedroom   storeroom
3. piano   armchair   fireplace   bookcase   telephone   radiator
4. plasticine   crayon   marbles   computer   football   microscope   puzzle
5. (a) Can we go out on the balcony?   (b) This house is really beautiful!
6. (a) downstairs   (b) upstairs   (c) upstairs   (d) downstairs

EXERCISE BOOK 練習冊

P.1

1. 略

2. (a) four windows   (b) three windows

P.2

1. Yes, it is.   2. Yes, it is.   3. No, it isn't.
4. No, it isn't.   5. Yes, it is.   6. No, it isn't.

P.3

1. dining room   2. kitchen   3. study
4. bathroom   5. storeroom   6. living room

P.4

1. F   2. A   3. D   4. B   5. I   6. E   7. J   8. C   9. H   10. G

P.5

1. true   2. true   3. false   4.true   5. false   6. true

P.6

略

P.7

1. piano   2. bookcase   3. bed   4. playroom